SCRATCH KITTEN
and the
TREASURE ISLAND

For Annabel—JG

For Mike, Rita, Che, Joel and Leah—MV

SCRATCH KITTEN
and the
TREASURE ISLAND

JESSICA GREEN • MITCH VANE

LITTLE  HARE
www.littleharebooks.com

Little Hare Books
8/21 Mary Street, Surry Hills
NSW 2010 AUSTRALIA

www.littleharebooks.com

First published in 2009

National Library of Australia
Cataloguing-in-Publication entry

Green, Jessica.

Scratch Kitten and the treasure island / Jessica Green ;
illustrator Mitch Vane.

978 1 921541 06 3 (pbk.)

For primary school age.

Vane, Mitch.

A823.4

Cover design by Lore Foye
Set in 17/24 pt Bembo by Clinton Ellicott
Printed in China by C&C Offset Printing Co. Ltd.

5 4 3 2 1

Contents

How It All Began

Scratch had sailed with pirates, escaped hungry sharks and rescued a captain from an icefloe. Now he sat on the prow of the *Jaunty Jessie*, purring as it docked. The boat had a huge haul of herring, and once it was unloaded, Scratch and his friend Jock would head back to sea.

But as the *Jaunty Jessie* drew
alongside the wharf, Scratch noticed
another ship at anchor. What he saw
was more exciting than any of his
adventures.

It wasn't that the ship was pink,
with lovely pink sails. It was the
ginger cat perched on the prow.
A big ginger cat with a straggly tail
and three legs!

'Paa!'

Forgetting Jock and the *Jaunty Jessie*, Scratch leapt for the pink ship. He stretched out his claws and hooked onto a rope that dangled from its rail.

Jock jumped up and down. 'Cat overboard!' he called. 'Come back, Ginger!'

Scratch began clawing up the rope.
'Sorry, Jock!' he yowled. 'But that's
my long-lost Paa up there! Thanks
for everything, Jock, but I have to go
with my Paa!'

'Come back!' Jock cried again.

But Scratch kept climbing until
he tumbled onto the deck of the
pink ship.

1.

A Very Pink Ship

Scratch shook himself and looked around for Paa. He could hardly see anything because of all the sailors bustling about in their smart maroon trousers and jackets.

Scratch blinked. The sailors were all women. He'd never met a lady sailor before.

Paa limped between the sailors.

'I *knew* you looked familiar!' he exclaimed. 'But which one are you? Chat? Brat?'

'I'm *Scratch*. Don't you remember?'

'You're the one who kept getting into mischief!'

'But I'm grown up now, Paa . . .'

'And what are you doing here?'

'I want to sail with you, Paa,' Scratch mewed. 'I'm a good ship's cat and you'll be so proud of me! I've sailed icy seas, been a pirate's cat and . . .'

'Scruffy little fellow, aren't you?' growled Paa. 'Hair all over the place, and look at that salty tail!

You'd better get back to your own ship before Mrs Captain sees you.'

'But, Paa, I've just found you!'

'It isn't as simple as that. You can't stay just because you want to. Everything has to be *just right* on board the *Just Right*!'

Scratch gave his salty tail a quick lick. 'I can be "just right"!' he mewed, and licked some more. 'See?'

Paa nudged Scratch away from a passing sailor's polished boots. 'You have to keep your wits about you, too,' he said. 'Follow me.'

All around them sailors worked at top speed. Paa squeezed between two stacks of crates. Scratch squeezed in behind him.

'Ahoy there, Crow's Nest
Caroline!' cried a sailor who was
trying to lash some ropes to the
foremast. 'Give me a hand!'

'I don't have time, Mainsheet
Mandy,' muttered Crow's Nest
Caroline. 'I have to scrub the
crow's nest.'

She scrambled up the rope ladder, her long plait swinging down her back.

'I'm Caroline's mate,' Paa explained to Scratch. 'Sometimes she takes me up there to share the watch. But mostly I watch from the bowsprit. It's hard for me to climb the rigging.'

'I could help you, Paa! I'm a good climber!'

Paa didn't seem to hear. 'There's no pleasing Mrs Captain,' he said. 'Just when you think you know all the rules . . .'

Suddenly he stopped and growled softly.

The sailors worked even harder.

A tiny, bent old woman was marching along the deck. The top of her grey head was no higher than the sailors' shoulders, her face was as wrinkled and brown as a walnut, and she had glaring ice-blue eyes.

'Girls!' she screeched. 'This ship must leave in an hour!'

Mainsheet Mandy gasped. 'But Mrs Captain, ma'am,' she whimpered, blinking tears from her eyes, 'you said we'd have shore leave . . .'

'I said, I said!' Mrs Captain screeched even louder. 'Plans have changed! Now I say we're sailing! There will be plenty of time for shore leave when we find what we're looking for!'

She stamped her foot and the
sailors shook with terror.

'See, Scratch?' Paa sighed. 'Go back
to your own ship. Life is too tricky
aboard the *Just Right*!'

'I'm not going!' Scratch miaowed.
'I want to sail with you!'

Mrs Captain suddenly stooped
to glare between the crates.

'What's this?' she cried. '*Another* cat?'

'Paa's my pa!' Scratch mewed.

Mrs Captain ignored him. 'He looks like you, Old Thomas!' she shouted. 'But is he a good worker?'

'I'm a fine ship's cat,' Scratch mewed. 'Just like Paa.'

'Where did the noisy little beast come from?' Mrs Captain yelled.

She grabbed Scratch, dangled him by the scruff of his neck and scowled into his face. Paa crept further back. The sailors trembled.

'We don't know where he sprang from,' said Mandy, 'but he looks a useful little fellow.'

Crow's Nest Caroline called from the rigging. 'That's right, ma'am!

Poor Thomas is not so good at climbing. The kitten could share Lookout Duty.'

'Very well,' said Mrs Captain, dropping Scratch to the deck. 'He can learn the rules for when Thomas pops his clogs.'

She stomped off to the bridge. The sailors breathed sighs of relief.

Paa crept out from hiding. 'Pop my clogs, indeed!' he growled. '*Nobody* can take my place on the *Just Right*! Not even you, son!' He stalked to the bow and jumped to his favourite spot on the bowsprit.

Scratch was left alone on the deck.

2.

Scratch Learns the Rules

He wasn't alone for long. The sailors clustered around him. He was picked up by a woman called Scurvy Sue, who had a big nose and bigger ears.

Sue cuddled him close as she tickled his ears. 'He really is a tiny Thomas!' she cried.

'Except he's grown a new leg and lost weight!' said Long-legs Lol.

Lol was so tall and thin that Sue's nose bumped her elbow.

A short, fat sailor called Anchor Annie reached out her plump arms. 'Let *me* hold him!' she said.

Scratch squirmed as he was passed from sailor to sailor. Paa scowled out to sea. The sailors were so busy cuddling Scratch they didn't notice Mrs Captain coming back.

'What's this?' she hollered. She glared at Scratch. 'What are *you*

doing here? Haven't you learnt
the rules? Rules are rules! And the
first rule, Young Tiger, is to obey
the rules!'

Scratch was dumped on the deck.
The sailors scurried back to work.

Scratch rubbed against Mrs
Captain's legs. He wanted to thank
her for letting him stay on board.
But suddenly he was bowling along
the deck. Mrs Captain had shoved
him with the tip of her boot.

'Next rule!' she shouted. 'No
sitting around purring! Look at
Old Thomas here! He's working!'

Paa's tail swished and his ears
twitched.

'Aye, Mrs Captain, ma'am!' yowled
Scratch. 'I'm a good ship's cat!'

'Another rule!' Mrs Captain
yowled back. 'Quit yowling!'

With a final glare she stomped to
the bridge.

Paa looked over his shoulder.
'Best if you hide a while, son,' he
growled, 'until she gets cross with
someone else!'

'But how do I stop her getting
cross with me again?' Scratch mewed.

'That's the hard part,' said Paa.

'You have to follow all her rules.'

Scratch slunk into the shadows between the crates. 'How many rules are there on this ship?' he wondered. 'And will I ever be able to learn them?'

3.

Scratch Breaks the Rules

Scratch hid until the ship left harbour. Before long he felt the ship heave on the swell, and heard waves slap against the bow. He was worried about the rules, but it felt good to be back at sea, even though he had to leave Jock behind on the *Jaunty Jessie*.

'Perhaps Mrs Captain has forgotten about me,' he thought.

He crept out from the crates and padded along the deck. A sailor stood at the helm, and a few sailors manned the rigging. Mrs Captain was nowhere to be seen. Keeping an eye out for her, he wandered down the hatch and found the galley. Grizzly Griselda stood at the stove, grizzling and moaning. She sounded just like Scratch's first sailor-friend, Peg-leg!

Scratch mewed.

'Stop nagging,' Grizzly Griselda snarled at him, 'and get out of my way or I'll dump you in the scuttlebutt. That's where I throw *anything* that annoys me.'

Scratch scampered through a door into the dining mess. Most of the crew were at the table, scrubbed and fresh in pink trousers and frilly blouses, eating stew and bread and butter.

Mrs Captain sat at the head of the table. Her hands were so well scrubbed that they gleamed like bones. She was showing the girls how to hold a spoon while keeping their little fingers in the air. Her chin didn't reach the table top, so only her eyes, nose and grey bun of hair were visible.

'So this is where you all are!' Scratch mewed.

No one heard, because Mrs Captain was busy shouting orders.

'Get your elbows off the table, you savage!' she bawled at Scurvy Sue.

'Look at you, Anchor Annie, dripping stew down your chin! Use your napkin!' Mrs Captain rapped her spoon on the table, spattering gravy on the cloth. 'Mandy, did you scrub your fingernails? The rule is, scrub your hands before meals!'

'But you said to save water!' Mandy whimpered.

Scratch darted under the table for a quick wash. Mrs Captain might want to inspect his claws!

'Rules are rules!' Mrs Captain screeched. 'To marry a seagoing gentleman, like I did, you need scrubbed fingernails!'

Scratch was worried about his dirty paws, but the aroma of stew made

him careless. He jumped onto a
chair. Scurvy Sue was already sitting
on it, but she didn't mind. She even
slipped him a chunk of meat.

Scratch should have stayed quiet
because just then Mrs Captain
ran out of breath and stopped
shouting. But the stew was so
tasty he couldn't help purring.

He purred so loudly that Mrs Captain heard. She peered over her plate and saw him chewing with his mouth open. Her eyes popped.

'The rule is,' she screeched, 'cats don't sit on laps! Why aren't you on watch with Thomas?'

Scratch jumped off Sue's lap and slunk up to the foredeck. 'If I can't sit at the table,' he thought, 'and if the cook doesn't like me, how will I eat?'

'So, you've been in strife twice!' said Paa from the bowsprit. 'You should have gone back to your ship when you had the chance. Now you're stuck here until *she* finds *him*. You'd better start pleasing *her* or it'll be more trouble for *you*!'

'*How* do I please her?' mewed Scratch.

'Like she said: follow the rules,' Paa growled. 'If you can keep up with them!'

'And what sort of trouble?' Scratch wailed.

Paa didn't answer. He smoothed his whiskers, jumped down from the bowsprit and went to stare out to sea from the top of a barrel.

4.
Looking Busy

Next morning, Scratch woke to
scraping sounds. He peeked out
from between the crates and saw
Lol hauling a telescope along the
port side of the deck. Scurvy Sue
already had one set up. Another
two telescopes were on the starboard
side. Anchor Annie was standing
on a box to peer through one, and

Mainsail Mandy was looking through the other.

Paa was at the bowsprit, gazing out to sea.

Scratch jumped up behind him. 'What is everyone looking at, Paa?' he asked. 'Icebergs? Pirates?'

'We're not looking *at* anything,' said Paa. 'We're looking *busy*. It's a rule. Haven't you learnt yet? We're searching for Mrs Captain's husband.'

Scratch was getting confused. 'There's a *Mr* Captain?'

'Captain Bluff. She's been searching for twenty years. And she won't stop till she's found him.'

'Where is he?' asked Scratch.

'If she knew, she wouldn't be
searching!' Paa snapped. 'People tell
her of sightings and she follows trails.
The last she heard is he's got an island
hideaway, so now we're searching
for *that*.'

'Mrs Captain must love him very
much to search for so long!'

'She doesn't want *him*! She wants
what he stole!'

'What's that, Paa?'

Paa took a quick look around. 'Keep staring out to sea, in case *she's* about,' he warned. 'Look at the horizon. Move your head from side to side. Look busy.'

Scratch looked as busy as he could.

'Bluff was a sea captain,' Paa said. 'He married Mrs Captain, but he couldn't keep up with her rules.

So he stole her special treasure and ran away. She's been chasing him ever since.'

'What special treasure?'

'The Pink Pebble Diamonds,' whispered Paa. 'The finest diamonds ever found.'

'So we're on a treasure hunt!' Scratch squeaked.

'*I'm* on a treasure hunt,' Paa growled. '*You* aren't, until you show you're a good worker. You know what happens if you don't obey the rules?'

Scratch wobbled nervously on the bowsprit. 'Does she biff you? Or put you in the scuttlebutt?'

'Worse. She drops you down the

Black Hole,' said Paa. 'That's the hatch where Grizzly Griselda keeps her coal. It's so black in there you can't see a thing. All you hear are waves slapping against the hull.'

Scratch whimpered to himself. There were many dangers aboard the *Just Right*. If you annoyed Grizzly Griselda, you went in the scuttlebutt.

If you disobeyed the rules, you went in the Black Hole.

So he pricked his ears and turned his head from side to side, staring popeyed first one way and then the other, and clinging dizzily to the bowsprit.

5.

Scratch Tries
to Please

Scratch was so busy looking busy
that he didn't see Mrs Captain
coming with her telescope under
her arm.

'Why is Young Tiger daydreaming
up there with you, Old Thomas!' she
yelled. 'It's not allowed! It's the rules!
He should be watching for *signs*
through the scuppers at all times.

Signs of seeds, twigs, or leaves,
anything that shows we're near an
island.'

Mrs Captain screwed one eye shut
and looked through her telescope.
'Where *are* you?' she muttered,
scanning the horizon.

'I'm here, ma'am!' Scratch mewed.
'Watching for twigs!'

Mrs Captain took no notice of him. 'Is that a smudge ahead?' she said. 'A ship? Bluff's Island?'

'I don't see a smudge,' Scratch said. 'Have you licked that spyglass clean?'

'Stop caterwauling!' cried Mrs Captain. 'The rule is: cats don't yowl. Now get away with you!'

'Go on then,' growled Paa. 'Watch through the scuppers!'

'But, Paa, you said to watch the horizon!'

'That was this morning. *Now* the rule is to watch the water.'

Scratch jumped down and scampered to a scupper.

'Useless as an anchor without a chain!' Mrs Captain snarled at him.

'If Old Thomas doesn't teach you the rules, quick smart, you'll *both* spend a day in the Black Hole!'

Scratch poked his head through the scupper to stare at the water. His ears and whiskers drooped with worry. He had to please Mrs Captain! But how could he get the rules right when they kept changing?

Scratch wanted to stay near Paa. But when Paa was sent to watch from the scuppers, Scratch was sent to watch from the bridge. Then Mrs Captain changed her mind and said, 'No cats on the bridge! That's the rule! Watch for signs from the bow!'

Scratch watched the horizon from

the bridge and the bow and the
scuppers and the prow until he
thought his eyes would fall out.
When Mrs Captain saw his eyelids
drooping she screamed, 'the rule is:
cats watch day and night! Cats have
good night eyes and have to watch
for signs!'

When night came, Scratch was worn out. The rules had changed so many times his head spun, and his paws ached from scuttling from one end of the ship to the other. He needed food and sleep. Most of all, he needed Paa.

Scratch found Paa sitting with his head poking through a scupper. It looked as if he was staring at the water, but Scratch heard snoring. Paa was looking busy and sleeping at the same time.

Scratch tried to do the same. But thoughts of the Black Hole kept him awake for a long time.

6.

Play It By Ear

'What are the rules today?' Scratch
asked Paa next morning.

'Don't know, son,' said Paa. 'Play it
by ear.'

He limped off to the galley to beg
Grizzly Griselda for fish.

Scratch dared not follow in case he
broke a rule. Instead he gave his ears
a wash. Paa said to play it by ear.

So it must be important to have
clean ears, even if his claws were
still a bit dirty.

Scratch was so busy licking that he
didn't hear Mrs Captain until it was
almost too late. He stuck his head
out through a scupper just in time,
and pricked his ears in a listening,
busy way.

'Now she'll see how busy I am!' he thought.

Mrs Captain stopped behind him. 'You aren't going to spot islands by staring through a scupper!' she cried. 'You're as useless as a cask with a hole in it! Get up to the crow's nest! That's the rule!'

Scratch's clean ears drooped as he stared up at the mast.

'Go on! What are you waiting for?' screeched Mrs Captain.

Scratch leapt to the rigging and climbed up to the crow's nest.

The sun shone and the sea glistened. Gulls squealed, dolphins frolicked and whales breached.

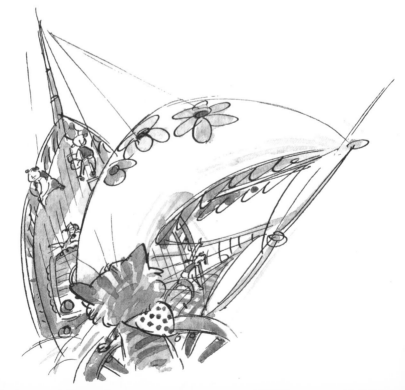

But no island came into view, so Scratch said nothing. Far below, Paa stared out to sea from the bowsprit, while Scurvy Sue, Mainsail Mandy, Long-legs Lol and Crow's Nest Caroline peered through the telescopes.

Hours passed. No one came up to help Scratch. He grew hungry, bored and lonely. His eyelids started to droop. He leaned against the brass rail and did what Paa did: he looked busy and dozed.

On the deck, Mrs Captain was bossing the sailors. 'Gentlemen sailors like shipshape ships, girls,' she screeched. 'You must polish the brass fittings while you're on watch.

This ship has to gleam like pink diamonds and gold. Crow's Nest Caroline, Young Tiger will help you!'

Scratch blinked awake at the sound of his name. 'Nothing to report, ma'am!' he mewed sleepily.

'And while you're on watch,' Mrs Captain went on, 'report any sign of an island! Especially an island shaped like a crouching cat. There'll be jam roly-poly for the first to spot it!'

Caroline climbed up to the crow's nest with her polishing cloths, and Scratch watched the horizon while Caroline polished. His tummy rumbled at the thought of jam roly-poly.

At last, far off to port side, Scratch

saw something. It looked like a hump in the water, but was it an island or an iceberg? And was it shaped like a cat? Scratch's tail puffed. Here was his chance to please Mrs Captain.

'*Miiaowww!*' he cried.

'Young Tiger has seen something!' Caroline shouted.

The crew rushed to the rail.

On the bridge, Mrs Captain swung her telescope around. 'All I see is a whale!' she screeched. 'The rule is: report signs of an island only!'

The sailors scurried back to watching and polishing. They didn't want to be caught whale watching!

Scratch's clean ears drooped even further.

'Never mind!' said Caroline. 'You're trying your best.'

But Scratch did mind. He was so muddled he didn't know what to report or what not to report. What if he cried 'island' and it was another whale? What if the whale was really a ship? What if no one believed him?

Then he noticed another smudge. But what sort of a smudge was it? He had seen smudges before. Sometimes they were storm clouds, or whales, or ragged reefs, or icefloes, or pirate ships. None had been an island. Perhaps this wasn't an island either.

The smudge slowly floated nearer.

'Islands don't float!' Scratch thought. 'Lucky I didn't shout!'

'Drat!' Caroline muttered. 'Where is my spyglass? Not in my pocket. Not down my shirt. I must have left it in the galley. I hope Grizzly Griselda didn't throw it in the scuttlebutt! Keep watch, Tiger. And don't report anything but islands!'

Scratch watched the smudge. It was like a dark thundercloud, with dark blue sails and a dark blue hull. It was a ship, and on its flag, fluttering in the breeze, was the picture of a pile of pink rocks.

Scratch looked back to the horizon. He had to watch for islands. Not ships.

7.

The Black Hole

Scratch heard Caroline return, but he didn't look around. He was busy watching for islands.

Suddenly there was a gasp. Scratch turned around. It wasn't Caroline at all. It was Mrs Captain, and she was staring at the dark blue ship.

'A ship!' she gasped. 'I came up to inspect the brass and I see a ship!

Why didn't you say something?
I told you to report everything!
You useless animal!' She bellowed
to the sailors below. 'The *Sea Scourer*
to starboard!'

Suddenly sailors were running
about like ants, pulling on ropes,
hauling at the capstan, scrambling up
and down the rigging. By the time

Mrs Captain reached the deck, the
Just Right had changed course and
was chasing the blue ship.

Mrs Captain hopped up and down
on the bridge 'Faster, girls! Faster!
Hoist all sails!' she screamed. 'Come
back here, Captain Bluff! I want a
word with you!'

Scratch cowered in the crow's nest. No matter what he did, he got it wrong. It would be the Black Hole for him!

In the meantime, the *Sea Scourer* changed direction and drew away.

For hours the two ships lumbered through the waves. When the *Sea Scourer* headed west, the *Just Right* followed. When the *Sea Scourer* turned east, so too did the *Just Right*. All afternoon the chase dragged on.

Then, as night fell, the blue ship melted into the darkness.

Mrs Captain was furious. She sent Caroline to fetch Scratch.

'This is your fault!' she scolded. 'You ignored a ship right in front of

your nose! The rule is to report
anything you see!'

She grabbed Scratch by his scruff
and stamped along the deck. Scratch
squirmed wildly. Mrs Captain held
tight and tramped down the steps
below deck, along a passage, around
corners, and down more steps.

At last, in the darkest part of the ship, she came to a hatch.

'Not the Black Hole!' Scratch mewed, wriggling even harder. 'Paa, help me!'

Mrs Captain heaved the hatch open. Beneath it was a yawning black hole.

'No!' Scratch squealed.

No one came to help.

But as Scratch fell into the darkness, he glimpsed a ragged ginger tail disappearing behind some barrels.

Then the hatch slammed shut and everything went black.

8.
Scratch Spots a Sign

Scratch crouched in the dark. For a long time he didn't dare move. After a while he blinked his eyes. But no matter how hard he blinked, he saw only blackness.

Then he heard the swishing sound of the ship slicing through the waves.

'Paa said to play it by ear,' he thought. 'Maybe this is what he meant.'

Scratch washed his ears again, in case he needed them.

He waited some more, listening to the swish of water against the hull.

He had no way of telling how long he had been in there.

Up on deck, Scurvy Sue was supposed to be measuring the depth of the water. But she was tired and

sad. The sailors had worked for hours chasing the blue boat, and she had wept many tears for the poor kitten in the Black Hole. She rubbed her nose on her sleeve.

'I'm too sad to do this,' she snivelled. 'I'll just write down the same depth as last time. Mrs Captain won't notice.'

In the Black Hole, after what seemed like forever, Scratch noticed that the sounds were changing. First there had been slapping sounds. Now there were scraping sounds. Scratch washed his ears and listened again. The slapping sounds came from waves against the side of the hull.

But the scraping sounds came from down at the bottom of the hull.

'I wonder why the sounds have changed,' he said, blinking into the darkness. 'Maybe the new sounds are signs of islands! Or reefs!'

Perhaps the ship was scraping against the bottom of the ocean!

He scrambled around in the dark, stumbling and slipping on the loose coal. 'Help!' he howled. 'Let me out! There are signs!'

No one came.

But someone heard.

Paa had been sitting by the hatch, worrying about his scruffy son.
He felt cross with himself. He hadn't tried very hard to help Scratch with

the rules, and now Scratch was in the
Black Hole.

When he heard Scratch yowling he
knew something was wrong.

Paa hobbled to the deck, where
Caroline was diving for her telescope
in the scuttlebutt.

'That Griselda!' she muttered.

'How will I ever be able to see
through this?'

Paa yowled and clawed at her legs.

'What is it?' asked Caroline.

Paa miaowed and hobbled back
below, stopping and looking over his
shoulder to make sure Caroline
followed.

'What's the matter?' she asked.

Then she heard Scratch yowling.

'Poor little Tiger!' she cried. She opened the hatch and hauled him out.

Scratch clawed up her arm. To Scratch the night seemed as bright as day after the darkness of the Black Hole.

'I must report to Mrs Captain,' he squealed as he dashed off.

Paa and Caroline followed as Scratch scampered to the bridge, but Mrs Captain wasn't there. Scratch scampered fore, and then aft, but she wasn't there either. He galloped back below decks to Mrs Captain's cabin and jumped on her bed, leaving sooty black marks on her quilt.

Mrs Captain wasn't there.

Scratch ran on to the dining mess. The table was set for breakfast. He left showers of sooty fur across the white cloth, but Mrs Captain wasn't there.

Meanwhile, Mrs Captain came down from the crow's nest, where she had been on watch. By the light of the ship's lantern she saw the black paw-prints all over the deck.

'Cat prints! Coal dust! How did he get out? Wait till I get my hands on Young Tiger!' she yelled.

The paw prints led her to the bow, where Scratch stood on the rail, yowling into the night. Paa yowled through a scupper close by.

Caroline was swishing her telescope wildly across the horizon looking for signs, but all she could see was scuttlebutt water.

'Filthy animal! The rule is: wash and work! Wash and . . . what's that?' Mrs Captain stared to starboard, where a dark shadow loomed in the night. A yellow star twinkled at the top of the shadow.

'Ship!' Scratch yowled.

Mrs Captain blinked. 'That's a lantern!' she bellowed. 'And that's a ship!'

'And an island!' Scratch yowled.

'And Bluff's Island!' roared Mrs Captain. 'All hands on deck!'

9.
Treasure Island

Mrs Captain ordered the sailors to anchor the *Just Right* alongside the *Sea Scourer*.

'I'm going to give Captain Bluff the fright of his life!' she said.

When dawn arrived, they saw a plume of smoke rising from the beach. Mrs Captain and some of the sailors boarded a rowboat.

They were about to give Captain Bluff a wake-up call he'd never forget. Paa and Scratch jumped into the rowboat too.

'To shore!' Mrs Captain growled.

The sailors rowed as hard as they could.

Captain Bluff's sailors lay around a bonfire on the beach. Some sprawled

on their backs, others curled into balls. One lay on his belly with his head inside an empty keg. Two sailors quarrelled over a sandcastle.

'I want to build battlements!' cried one.

'No! I want it to have turrets!' cried the other.

They didn't notice the pink rowboat arrive, or the lady sailors jumping out to beach it.

'Bluff!' Mrs Captain suddenly roared. 'Show yourself!'

The castle builders gaped, then dived behind their castle. The other men snored on. There was no answer from Captain Bluff. Mrs Captain marched up the beach.

'Bluff!' Mrs Captain bellowed. 'I want a word with you! Where are my diamonds?'

One of the castle builders popped up his head and peered towards a grove of trees.

'Aha! Come along, Sue and Lol!' Mrs Captain cried. 'Annie, Caroline, Griselda, keep an eye on these ruffians!'

She stamped toward the trees. Scratch quickly washed his whiskers and ears and followed. After all, he was the one who had sounded the alarm. Paa stayed by the fire, sniffing for fish.

Mrs Captain was in such a hurry, she stumbled three times in the sand.

By the time she reached the grove,
her hat had fallen off and her hair was
unravelling. But she didn't seem to
care. She had found Captain Bluff!

He was asleep in a hammock
strung between two trees. He wore
a blue peaked cap and big, scuffed
boots. His buttons were open and
his scarf and belt were undone.

In his arms he cradled an ebony
walking cane.

Mrs Captain reached out and
swung the hammock so hard it spilled
Captain Bluff onto the ground.
He lay sprawled on his back, spitting
out sand. One hand still clutched
his cane.

'Well, Bluff?' said Mrs Captain.

'Why, hello ... dear,' he spluttered.
'Didn't expect to see you here!'

'Where's my treasure?'

Bluff struggled to sit up.
'T-t-treasure?' he said, rubbing his
hands on the silver handle of his
cane. 'You're my only treasure,
my dear.'

'Where is it?' Mrs Captain roared.

'Would you believe that it was washed overboard in a great typhoon?'

'No, I wouldn't!'

'Neither would we!' cried Sue.

'Nor me!' mewed Scratch.

'Well, how about . . . I was polishing the diamonds on deck one day, when a huge tentacle reached out of the water and——'

'*Where's my treasure?*' bawled Mrs Captain.

Bluff struggled to his feet and leant on his cane. 'The truth is,' he grunted, 'we were raided by pirates only a month after I last saw you. I've been trying to find something special for you ever since.'

'Really?' said Mrs Captain.

'Really?' said Sue and Lol.

'Really!' mewed Scratch.

Bluff smirked. 'Really,' he said.

Mrs Captain's shoulders drooped
and her hands fell to her sides.
'Do you mean my diamonds are
gone forever?' she asked.

Captain Bluff twirled his cane and
grinned. 'I'm afraid so, dear,' he said.

Mrs Captain brushed a tear from
her eye. 'Oh! Well! I . . .'

Scratch rubbed against Mrs
Captain's leg.

Captain Bluff patted Mrs Captain
on the head. 'So run along home,
and I'll find you a nice coral
necklace, eh?'

Mrs Captain turned to leave. 'Let's go,' she mumbled.

Sue and Lol put their arms around Mrs Captain to help her back to the beach.

Captain Bluff smirked again and dug the tip of his cane into the sand. 'Good riddance!' he muttered.

'Miaow!' mewed Scratch angrily. 'You're a mean man!'

He lunged at Bluff and dug his claws into his leg. Bluff lurched backwards and fell over. The cane snapped in two under his weight.

Suddenly something small and pink and sparkly bounced around Scratch's paws. A stream of glittering little rocks was spilling out from the hollow end of Captain Bluff's broken cane!

'Mrs Captain!' Scratch miaowed.

Captain Bluff struggled to his knees. He crawled towards Scratch and the bouncing pink rocks.

Mrs Captain kept stumbling towards the beach.

'Treasure ahoy!' Scratch yowled. He leapt onto Bluff's back and dug his claws in deep.

Lol looked over her shoulder. She saw Scratch on Bluff's back. Then she saw the glittering pink stones on the ground.

'Mrs Captain!' she shouted. 'Look!'

Mrs Captain gasped. 'My diamonds!

She and Sue and Lol came running back. Captain Bluff tried to crawl away, but Scratch clawed his head.

'Thief!' Mrs Captain screamed. She grabbed one half of the cane and started hitting Captain Bluff with it. *Thump!* 'Liar!' *Whack!* 'Cheat!' *Bam!*

Bluff struggled to his feet, but without his cane, he couldn't run. Lol and Sue caught him and stood him before Mrs Captain. Then they gathered up the pink diamonds while Captain Bluff got a very long lecture about rules.

How It All Ended

The *Just Right* lay at anchor in the bay, clean and polished and ready to sail. Captain Bluff had promised to mend his wicked ways, and the *Sea Scourer* was also ready to leave.

Mrs Captain had said goodbye to Annie and Caroline. They had met two of Captain Bluff's sailors and had decided to marry them.

They would all live on the *Sea Scourer*.

Even Griselda had found someone to marry. It was Captain Bluff's cook.

'Poor Peg-leg needs me,' she grumbled. 'He only has one leg.'

Behind the sandcastle, Paa and Scratch washed themselves in readiness for the trip. Paa stretched each of his three legs, one at a time, to wash them. Scratch stretched and licked, too, leaving one leg unwashed. It felt rude to show off his fourth leg when Paa didn't have one.

'Good work, son!' said Paa. 'I always knew you'd make a great ship's cat.'

Scratch purred proudly. Mrs Captain had promised he could stay

on board the *Just Right* for ever, no matter how long it took for Paa to pop his clogs. Scratch had never been so happy.

Paa gave himself a shake. 'I'm going aboard the *Sea Scourer* now. Are you coming?'

'You mean the *Just Right*!' said Scratch.

Paa shook his head. 'I'm going with Grizzly Griselda. She's marrying a peg-legged cook. I'll feel more at home with someone who's lost a leg.'

'But I've only just found you!' Scratch miaowed.

'You don't need your paa now,' said Paa. 'You've proved you're a proper ship's cat. I'll see you around, eh?'

Paa hobbled down the beach to the *Sea Scourer*'s rowboat. He jumped on board and stood at the stern, his tail held high in farewell.

'Goodbye, Tiger!' cried Griselda. 'Remember the rules!'

'Goodbye, goodbye,' cried Annie and Caroline.

Scratch followed them to the

water's edge. He bravely held his own
tail high and watched as Paa was
rowed away.

Then he crept up the beach and
hid behind a tree. He needed time
to calm his wobbly paws, wash his
drooping whiskers, and get used to
the idea of life without Paa. Then
he would go aboard the *Just Right*.

But when he finally went back to the beach, it was very quiet.

And the bay was empty.

The *Sea Scourer* had sailed.

And so had the *Just Right*.

Scratch had been left behind on the island!

He ran back and forth along the shore, staring out to sea and mewing. But no one heard him.

He was all alone.

Not far out to sea, a bulky old barque lurched through the waves, headed for unknown waters. The captain of the *South Seas Explorer* didn't know where he was going, or what he would find when he got there.

But he did know that he and his crew would be at sea for a long, long time. And for such a long voyage, they needed fresh water. So he was very pleased when he saw a cat-shaped island on the horizon. Little did he know what he would find when he arrived.

And little did Scratch know what was in store . . .

Words Sailors Use

aft	at the back of a ship
barque	a sailing ship with three masts
bow	the forward part of a ship
bowsprit	a large pole that sticks out from the front of a ship
bridge	a raised platform where the sailor in charge navigates the ship
capstan	a device on a ship used to wind up the anchor cable
cask	a container shaped like a barrel, used for storing liquids
crow's nest	a small basket at the top of the mast, where a sailor could sit and look out for approaching land or danger
dining mess	the dining room on board a ship
dock	an area of calm water in a harbour where ships are moored
fore	at the front of the ship
foredeck	the deck at the front of a ship
foremast	the mast nearest the front of a ship
galley	a ship's kitchen
hatch	an opening in the ship's deck, covered by a watertight lid
helm	the big steering wheel on a sailing ship
hoist the sails	lift up the sails

hull	the frame of a ship
lookout	sailor who watches out for approaching hazards, other ships or land
mainsheet	the rope that controls the mainsail
mast	a stout pole rising straight up from the deck of a ship, which supports the yards and sails
on watch	to watch from the crow's nest for approaching hazards, other ships or land
port	sailor's word for 'left'
prow	the front part of a ship which is above the waterline
reef	rocks or coral found just below the surface of the sea
rigging	the ropes and chains used to move and support the sails on a ship
scupper	a drain hole on the deck
scuttlebutt	a water barrel on a ship, with a hole cut out, into which a sailor could dip his drinking cup
spyglass	a sailor's name for a small telescope
starboard	sailor's word for 'right'
stern	the rear part of a ship
swell	long, unbroken waves
typhoon	a very powerful tropical storm

About the Author

Jessica Green has always loved cats, and shares
her home with four furry feline friends—
Fang, Felis, Tre and Tumnus.

About the Artist

Mitch Vane would love to run away to sea
but she can't because after half an hour on a
boat she gets seasick!

Acknowledgements

Thanks to Michael, for trying, and failing,
to teach me to love the water.

Thanks to Nick, Richard and Gillian,
for assuring me that writing about mad
kittens is far more useful than a tidy house.

Thanks to Mitch, for seeing Scratch
so clearly.

Special thanks to Margrete, for planting the
idea of Scratch into my mind.

Jessica

For more exciting action with
the swashbuckling

SCRATCH KITTEN

look out for his other adventures . . .

SCRATCH KITTEN
GOES TO SEA

SCRATCH KITTEN
on the
PIRATE'S SHOULDER

SCRATCH KITTEN
and the
RAGGED REEF

SCRATCH KITTEN
and the
TERRIBLE BEASTIES

SCRATCH KITTEN
and the
GHOST SHIP